D1045700

DINOSAUR DETECTIVE CLUB

BOOK #1

The DISAPPEARANCE of Dinosaur Sue

Mackinac Island Press

for the love of reading

Other PaleoJoe Books

Dinosaur Detective Club Chapter Books

#2 Stolen Stegosaurus
Dinosaurs and danger are big adventure for
PaleoJoe and Shelly Brooks. Joined by fellow
schoolmate Dakota Jackson, Shelly and PaleoJoe
battle the dark side of fossil collecting while
making the greatest dinosaur discovery of all time.

Hidden Dinosaurs

...and more to come...

Text Copyright 2006 Joseph Kchodl
Illustration Copyright 2007 Mackinac Island Press, Inc.

Library of Congress Cataloging-in-Publication Data on file

PaleoJoe's Dinosaur Detective Club #1: The Disappearance of Dinosaur Sue

Summary: Eleven-year-old junior paleontologist Shelly helps PaleoJoe investigate the disappearance from Chicago's Field Museum of Dinosaur Sue, the most complete skeleton of a tyrannosaurus rex ever discovered.

ISBN 978-1-934133-03-3

Fiction
10 9 8 7 6 5 4 3 2

Printed and bound in the United States by Cushing-Malloy, Inc.

A Mackinac Island Press, Inc. publication
Traverse City, Michigan

www.mackinacislandpress.com

*Dedicated to the imagination
and discovery that
all children have with dinosaurs.*

THE
DISAPPEARANCE
OF
DINOSAUR
SUE

TABLE OF CONTENTS

TABLE OF CONTENTS

CHAPTER ONE

THE TOMBS

Creeek— squeeek— creeeek!

It was like music.

Swick—creeeky—squack!

The eighth step down was the best. Shelly Brooks rocked back and forth, back and forth between the seventh step and the eighth step savoring the delicious noise.

Squeeeky—squak—crik! Squeeeky— squak—crik! "Shelly Brooks, is that you or are we being invaded by monster beetles?" Mr. Summers, the museum security guard, poked his thin nose over the rail from the second landing high above Shelly.

Creek-
-squeeek-
-creeek

"Hi, Mr. Summers!" Shelly loved the way her voice echoed and bounced up and down the stairwell.

"Watch what you're doing on those old steps

11

and don't bother You-Know-Who!" But the warning was not stern and Shelly could hear Mr. Summers chuckle as he turned away.

Creeeky— swik— creeek— creeek!

Shelly continued her musical way down the stairs. Never walking when she could run, this was the only time in her day when Shelly permitted herself to slow down. You had to go slow to get the best creaks.

Shelly loved this old stairway that wound down deep into the depths of the Balboa Museum of Natural History. She felt like an explorer as she creaked her way into the dimness of the lower level—a level off limits to the visitors of the museum. A place called the Tombs.

At the bottom of the staircase a closed door blocked Shelly's way.

It was locked.

Suppressing a giggle because this was a game she loved to play, Shelly leaned against the wall next to the door. Out of her pocket she took a red yo-yo and began to spin it expertly up and down its string.

It wasn't long before the door opened and Bob, the maintenance chief, appeared. His tall, uniformed figure blocked the doorway.

"Miss Shelly Brooks," he said, and if he was smiling you couldn't tell because his face was hidden in a big black beard. "To gain entrance to the Tombs you must prove worthy by answering a question."

Carefully, Shelly put the yo-yo back in her pocket. She stood as straight as she could, her shoulders back, her short, red pony tail swaying as she tilted her head to look up at Bob. She was very serious.

What question would Bob have today?

Bob knew an awful lot. Being the museum's maintenance chief he knew every room and all its contents. Sometimes Shelly wondered if it was even possible that Bob knew more than her Gamma Brooks who conducted the museum tours and worked in the main office.

"No one enters the Tombs who cannot answer my question," Bob said, making his voice low and terrible.

"I'm ready," Shelly answered bravely.

"Name the best known sauropod."

Good. A dinosaur question! Shelly was an expert on all things dinosaur. She had read every book in the school library on dinosaurs and was currently working her way through the collection at the public library.

She knew the answer to this question instantly. But then, suddenly she had an idea. Why not see just how smart Bob was? She would try a little test of her own.

First, she would pretend she did not know the answer.

"Hmmm..." she frowned and scratched her head.

"Give up?" Bob began to close the door.

"No, wait! The answer is..." she paused to make sure she had Bob's full attention. She did. "*Apatosaurus*," she said clearly pronouncing each syllable.

For a minute she enjoyed the surprised look on Bob's face. He thought she had gotten it wrong!

"I'm sorry, Miss Shelly Brooks, but..."

"Which is another name," Shelly interrupted him, "for *Brontosaurus*."

A big grin broke through the black tangle of beard on Bob's face showing his big square teeth.

"You have answered correctly!" he said. "I must now stand aside and allow you to enter the Tombs."

And so he stood aside, holding the door open for Shelly.

"Enter, brave explorer, and search out the Unknown!"

Shelly stepped past him. He started to let the door close and then, as though remembering something important, he snatched it open.

"Oh, and don't bother You-Know-Who!" he warned, and as the door shut behind him, Shelly saw him give her a wink.

CHAPTER TWO

YOU-KNOW-WHO

Alone now, Shelly grinned at the stretch of empty hallway before her. As light on her feet as a bug skimmer on water, Shelly flew down the long corridor stopping at a closed door at the very end.

On the old frosted and speckled glass of the battered oak door hung a sign that said:

DO NOT DISTURB

But disturbing was what Shelly did best. Ignoring the sign, she turned the loose brown doorknob and opened the door.

At first all she could see was the clutter and

chaos of an over-full office. She could see stacks of books, scattered papers, boxes of rocks and stones, an old wasps' nest like a tattered paper bonnet on a twig, collection drawers of insects, and many, many bones.

And one person sitting at a desk who looked up from a large flat rock he was studying under a pool of white light and said, "Go away!"

"I can't," said Shelly. "I answered the 'Question' and was admitted to the Tombs. Now I am an explorer and you have to put up with me."

The man glared at the rock he was holding and said something that sounded like "Pish!"

Shelly hauled a rickety wooden stool from a corner and brought it over to the desk. Perched on it she had a good view of what the man was looking at.

She watched quietly for a few seconds while the man squinted at the rock, turning it this way and that in his strong hands. Dressed in olive green pants with the khaki sleeves of his shirt rolled over his elbows, his short, carefully trimmed graying beard giving him the face of an adventurer, Shelly knew that this man really was as glad to see her as she was to see him. This, too, was part of the game.

"What are you looking at?" she finally asked.

"A golf club," he answered, adjusting the magnifying glass he wore around his neck.

"Really? I think it's a fossil," said Shelly.

"Well, I'll be a *Pterodactyl's* uncle!" exclaimed the man. "How strange. What do you make of it then?"

Carefully, Shelly took the heavy stone from him and weighed it in her hands. It was a chipped and jagged piece of grayish-white stone. All across its surface, like miniature paintings in dark brown, were feathery plant-like images.

"It's beautiful!" Shelly exclaimed. "But I don't know what it is. I guess you'll have to tell me."

Which was what the man had been waiting for all along.

"You're right, Shelly," his voice was eager now, like that of a kid instead of a serious adult. "This is a fossil. See those feathery shapes? What do they look like to you?"

"They look like flowers."

"Yes, they do. People call them Lilies of the seas. But they are not plants, Shelly, they are animals!"

"Animals? They look like the skeletons of

Queen Anne's Lace." Shelly loved the lacy white flowers of Queen Anne's Lace and often picked handfuls of them in the ditches coming home from school to give to her Gamma Brooks.

"They are called crinoids," the man said. "They lived in ancient tropical seas millions of years ago. They lived in deep water. See?" Using a slender pointer the man showed the details of the fossil to Shelly. "This is the main part of the body where all the vital organs were. These feathery arms would wave about in the water and catch tiny plants and animals for the crinoid to eat."

"Wow!" Shelly smoothed the fossil gently with her fingers.

"Here. Take a closer look with the loupe," the man said, giving Shelly the magnifying glass.

As Shelly peered at the suddenly enlarged crinoid, the phone rang.

"I'll get it!" Shelly shouted as she catapulted off her stool sending it crashing to the floor. Holding the fossil in one hand she lunged for the phone scattering a handful of papers to the floor as she did so.

She caught it on the second ring. "Hello," she said. "You have reached the office of PaleoJoe, Dinosaur Detective."

"Pish," she heard PaleoJoe grumble as he picked up the fallen papers.

"Help!" said a breathless voice in Shelly's ear. "We need help at once!"

CHAPTER THREE

A CALL FOR HELP

Wide-eyed, Shelly handed the phone to Paleo-Joe. It wasn't often she found herself speechless, but what could one really say to such a desperate sounding plea? She quickly handed the phone to PaleoJoe.

"Hello?"

Shelly watched PaleoJoe's expression change from curiosity to alarm.

"What's gone missing?" PaleoJoe juggled the phone to his other ear as though that would allow him to hear better. "Sue?"

"Sue who? Is someone missing?" Shelly asked eagerly.

"No break-in?" PaleoJoe was now frantically searching for a piece of paper and a pencil to write with. His face was intent as he listened.

"Was it a robbery?" Shelly squeaked in excitement, completely ignoring PaleoJoe's flapping hand in her face for silence.

"No alarm went off then?" PaleoJoe covered the mouthpiece with his hand. "Quick, Shelly! Get me something to write with."

"Did they leave any fingerprints? Ask about fingerprints!" Shelly pushed a pencil and notepad at PaleoJoe.

"Quiet! I need to concentrate!" PaleoJoe snapped at her. "Oh no—I didn't mean you, Mr. Renfro. Please, go ahead."

Shelly sort of enjoyed the way PaleoJoe's face went red when he was embarrassed. Ignoring the glare he gave her, Shelly did nothing to quiet her eager dancing.

"Oh boy, a robbery!" she breathed, hugging herself in excitement.

"Uh-huh...uh-huh..." PaleoJoe tried to turn his back on her but only managed to get tangled up in the phone cord. "Sorry, can you repeat that? Right...no witnesses...uh-huh..."

"Jeeper peepers, a real robbery!" Shelly crowed hopping up and down. "We'll solve it! We can solve anything! The Great Detective and his faithful sidekick Shelly Brooks, Junior Paleontologist. Wow! A robbery!"

23

Keeping one ear tuned to PaleoJoe and his "uh-huhs," Shelly began digging in cupboards and pulling out various pieces of equipment.

"Let's see," she mumbled to herself as she dug into a drawer. "We'll want these for sure." She pulled out a battered rucksack and a small pink backpack. "We'll need this and these..." Carefully, she laid out an old battered cell phone, two notebooks and a handful of pencils, a magnifying glass and a handful of small plastic bags. Next she pulled out an ancient, well-thumbed copy of a book called *Dinosaurs of the World,* written by Amelia Cook Fogherty.

"I suppose he'll want to take that old thing," Shelly said to herself. "I don't know why. He knows all this stuff..." But she put the old book in the rucksack and then reached far into the back of a cupboard for one final item.

"Footprints...?" PaleoJoe said. Shelly was hardly listening.

We will definitely need this! Shelly thought to herself as she pulled out a small bundle of something that looked like rolled canvas. This bundle was PaleoJoe's tool roll–a cloth with many pockets to hold important dinosaur digging tools that rolled tightly and closed with a tie. But before she could put it into the rucksack she was startled into frozen, listening stillness.

"That's impossible!" PaleoJoe almost shouted.

He stood still, the phone pressed tight to his ear, listening hard. Was he still breathing? Shelly thought he looked pale.

"Are you absolutely sure about that?" he questioned his caller. His eyes were unfocused which always happened when he was thinking hard.

The next thing he said brought Shelly, breathless, the bundle forgotten on a chair, to stand close beside him straining to hear the distant voice on the other end of the phone.

"No," PaleoJoe gripped the phone. "Dinosaurs do not come back to life."

CHAPTER FOUR

DANGER-SMANGER

"What is it?" Shelly demanded, tugging at his arm. "What's going on?"

"I'll be there tomorrow," said PaleoJoe trying to shake her off. "Don't touch anything until I can get there. Good-bye, Mr. Renfro."

PaleoJoe hung up the phone.

PaleoJoe slowly let out his breath.

PaleoJoe sat down.

Shelly wanted to shake him!

"What!!??" she cried. "What's going on? Who was that? Was there a robbery?"

"Wait a minute, Shelly," PaleoJoe held up his

hand. "Let me think a minute."

"Not until you tell me everything!" And Shelly launched into Maximum Force Questioning—MFQ—in the face of which there is no known defense on the face of the planet. It was a technique which often proved successful when dealing with slow moving adults.

It sounded something like this:

"WhoisSueandwhatfootprintswhoisthisRenfrodudeisitarobberyfarawaydoyoureallythinkyouwillneedthatrattyolddinosaurbookbythatancientFoghertywomanwhendoweleave?"

"STOP!" PaleoJoe, caving under the pressure of MFQ, leaped to his feet waving his arms in the air.

"Okay, okay! I'll tell you all about it. What's that?" he said, pointing to the pink backpack lying innocently next to the battered rucksack.

"It's my backpack," said Shelly. "I'm getting us ready."

"Oh no you're not!" And PaleoJoe did not smile. He wasn't kidding. "You are not coming with me on this one, Shelly. It's too dangerous."

For an instant Shelly was actually shocked into silence.

"Of course I'm coming with you." Why did

27

PaleoJoe look so serious? She tried her dimply smile on him.

No luck.

"Not this time," said Ironface.

"Why not?" Maybe a strategic pout would work.

No luck.

"There are things about this case which I don't like," said the hard-hearted man. "It feels too dangerous. You can't come."

"Of course I can."

"No, you can't"

"Can."

"Can't!"

"Can!!"

"CANNOT. And stop that!" Sometimes, Paleo-Joe thought, it was hard to be an adult when you were around this little force known as Shelly Brooks.

"Give me one good reason," said Shelly reasonably. Really, sometimes PaleoJoe was just like a little kid.

"You have school."

"It's Friday."

"It's too dangerous."

"Danger-smanger."

"That's not an argument," said PaleoJoe.

"Look, Shelly, this is big. Very big. Too big. I'm going alone."

Shelly could see that 'tactics' would be called for.

"Well," she said and tried to look disappointed. "At least let me help you pack."

"Thanks, but I can manage," said PaleoJoe smiling at her. "I'll tell you all about it when I get back."

"Okay," said Shelly sliding off her stool. "But promise me you will tell me everything."

"I promise," said PaleoJoe sincerely, but when he saw the angelic smile Shelly gave him he suddenly remembered how dangerous it could be to make promises to Shelly.

"Thanks for showing me the crinoid. See you later!"

PaleoJoe waved a hand at Shelly and turned away reaching for his phone, his mind already on other things. Quickly, as she passed the chair, Shelly scooped up the canvas tool roll and slipped it into her pink backpack, casually tossing it over her shoulder on her way out of the office.

When PaleoJoe looked up it was to see her ponytail disappear behind the closing door of his office.

CHAPTER FIVE

TACTICS

Bypassing the pleasure of creaks and squeaks, Shelly charged up the museum stairs at full speed. It was almost five o'clock–closing time.

In the small main lobby, weaving around the few remaining visitors, Shelly dashed into the front office. There she surprised the brilliantly blonde Annie, the museum secretary, who was just in the process of gathering up her things to go home.

"Oh! Hi, Shelly! You startled me." Annie had a bright dimply smile. When Shelly was a very little girl, she thought Annie must live in the sun because her blonde hair and friendly smile seemed to light her up like a summer day.

"Sorry, Annie. I had to catch you before you left."

"Well, you did. Now catch your breath and tell me what I can do for you."

"PaleoJoe needs Mr. Renfro's telephone number. He hoped you had it."

"PaleoJoe doesn't have The Field Museum's phone number?" Annie raised her perfect eyebrows in surprise.

"Well, you know PaleoJoe!" Shelly tried a chuckle. It didn't sound too fake, she decided.

"Yes, I know PaleoJoe. Smartest man this side of the Mississippi, but if his head wasn't attached it would roll away."

Maybe, Shelly thought gloomily, her little subterfuges were not putting PaleoJoe in the best light.

Annie ruffled through her index roll and wrote a number on a sticky note for Shelly.

"Here you go."

"Thanks!" Shelly took the number.

Dashing outside to wait on the front steps for Gamma Brooks, she looked thoughtfully at the phone number Annie had given her.

The Field Museum! Shelly knew all about

that magical place in Chicago. PaleoJoe had long promised to take her there someday. Shelly's favorite dream was to think of herself as a famous paleontologist who worked at The Field Museum.

And now that she knew Mr. Renfro was calling from The Field Museum, she began to suspect just what it was that had been stolen. PaleoJoe had not been joking when he said it was something big. In fact, if Shelly's suspicions were right, it was something very big indeed.

There was one way in which she could find out.

From her hip pocket Shelly dug out her cell phone. It was pink to match her backpack and also had a few more functions than PaleoJoe's ancient version. She flipped it open and punched in the number on the sticky note.

CHAPTER SIX

THE JABBERING JIBBIES

Shelly held the phone tight against her ear listening to the ringing.

"Field Museum. How can I help you?" a woman answered. The voice was nasal as though the operator was holding her nose as she spoke.

"Hello," said Shelly, holding her own nose. It would not be to her advantage to sound like an 11 year old girl. "This is the secretary from PaleoJoe's office. Could I please speak to Mr. Renfro?"

"One moment."

There was a pause filled by a very bad rendition of *Baby Elephant Walk* which Shelly recognized

because sometimes PaleoJoe would hum it while he worked. Impatiently Shelly tapped her fingers on the step and watched a series of small insects trying to figure out what the monolithic monster that was her shoe was doing in the middle of their world. One giant black ant had decided to try and scale her high-tops when the music cut out to be replaced by a harassed sounding voice.

"This is Renfro." Shelly recognized his voice as the same one which had called for help on Paleo-Joe's phone.

"Yes. Mr. Renfro, I'm calling from PaleoJoe's office. PaleoJoe just wanted me to double check on some details of this robbery." Shelly held her breath. Hopefully Mr. Renfro would tell her what she needed to know.

And, hopefully, her Gamma Brooks would not show up early.

"Right." Mr. Renfro sounded unsuspicious. "Robbery–if that's what you want to call it."

"Why? What would you call it?"

"Sorcery."

Shelly almost dropped her phone. "What!!??"

"Well, I mean, not really of course, but how would you explain the disappearance of the biggest *T. rex* skeleton in history from the heart of a well-secured, famous museum? And those footprints! I know what PaleoJoe said about them, but he hasn't seen them yet. I don't mind telling you they give me the jabbering jibbies."

 35

Which was sort of what the large black ant was currently giving Shelly, having found its way up her shoe and into the pant leg of her jeans.

"Oh!" gasped Shelly as she slapped her leg trying to annihilate the ant.

"Well, I don't mean to distress you," Mr. Renfro apologized.

"I'm not distressed," said Shelly distressed. It was hard to stay nasal without plugging her nose and that ant was truly making progress in the wrong direction.

"Anyway," continued Mr. Renfro, "like I told PaleoJoe, they look like authentic *T. rex* footprints. And there they are in that powdery white stuff that's all over the floor, looking like that great old exhibit just suddenly got up and walked away."

"Gosh!" Shelly's eyes widened at this bit of information and at the same time her fingers closed over the wiggly lump of ant in her pants near her knee.

"Yes, well, I told PaleoJoe all about that. They look authentic, but of course it's some sort of hoax."

Just then Shelly looked up to see Gamma Brooks emerge from the museum.

"Thank you, Mr. Renfro," she said hurriedly.

"I just needed to confirm PaleoJoe's arrival time."

"I'm expecting him on the ten o'clock flight in the morning. I'll have someone there to pick him up and bring him directly to the museum."

"Thank you. Good-bye." Shelly flipped her phone shut just as Gamma Brooks approached.

CHAPTER SEVEN

THE ULTIMATE UNDERCOVER PLAN

"Hi, Sweet Pea!" Gamma Brooks said. Her arms were loaded down with books, a heavy black purse slung over her shoulder, and a smile that was all crinkles and wrinkles. Gamma Brooks could write a dictionary of terms of endearment.

Shelly stood, and inventing some very interesting dance-like moves, she was able to extricate the sorry little crumpled form of the large black ant from her pant leg. She set it on the pavement and gently poked it with her finger. She was happy to see it un-stick itself and begin to totter off.

"Huh," said Gamma Brooks, watching. *"Myrmicinae* of the family *Formicidae*. Very sturdy fellows. Did it bite you?'

"No," Shelly said, taking an armful of books from Gamma.

"Female then," said Gamma Brooks. "Still capable of a pretty good tickle though, hey Honey-Pop?"

Together Shelly and Gamma Brooks began to walk down the street to the bus stop. The air was summer warm. In the amber sky overhead nighthawks swooped and dived on banded wings, dropping their peculiar call onto the evening stage.

Shelly bit her lower lip in concentration. Her hunch had to be right. After talking to Mr. Renfro, Shelly knew what had been taken from The Field Museum. She had to be involved with this case somehow.

What she needed was an Ultimate Undercover Plan. And she knew just the person who could help her with it.

Gamma Brooks.

If Gamma Brooks would ever discover extreme

 39

sports, Shelly felt certain her fearless grandmother would be at the front of it all with no consideration of age involved. Gamma was as far from the stereotyped knitting and baking grandmother as a person could be. She was a retired school teacher addicted to detective fiction and drama. She also knew pretty much everything there was to know about insects, which was why she volunteered a lot of her time at the Balboa.

"What's for supper tonight?" Shelly asked as they stood waiting for the bus. Sometimes Shelly spent the weekend at Gamma's.

"Oh, pig's wings on butterfly toast." Gamma Brooks gave her granddaughter a thoughtful look. "What's on your mind, little Chicken Liver?"

Only Gamma Brooks could turn chicken liver into an affectionate term, thought Shelly wrinkling her nose. "What do you know about Dinosaur Sue, Gamma?" she asked.

"Not as much as you probably," answered Gamma.

The bus pulled up and they got on, finding seats near the back. Gamma's apartment was about a ten minute ride from the museum.

"Tell me anyway," Shelly directed as they began their bouncy journey.

"Well, Sue is the largest and most complete fossil of a *T. rex* ever discovered. It is exhibited in The Field Museum in Chicago. The bones were discovered by a woman, Sue–someone–"

"Hendrickson," Shelly supplied.

"Yes. Sue Hendrickson. Which is why they call it Sue. Its skull is really big..."

"Five feet," said Shelly.

"Right," Gamma Brooks eyed the serious face of her granddaughter. "There were a lot of bones..."

"Over two hundred," said Shelly without blinking.

"Yes. Over two hundred. So what's up, Shellygoldfish?"

"Gamma, I think Sue has been stolen from The Field Museum."

"What?"

"And they called in PaleoJoe."

"Are you going with him?"

"He won't let me. He says it's too dangerous."

"Really?" Gamma questioned. The glint in Gamma Brook's eye might be described as 'dangerous' if it had been written in one of her detective stories.

The bus jolted to a stop. Gamma and Shelly

gathered up their belongings and got off. For a minute they stood on the sidewalk looking at each other.

"Have you ever been to The Field Museum?" Shelly asked.

"I have," said Gamma Brooks. "It's a splendid place. And I think you should see it."

"How about tomorrow?" asked Shelly.

"How about it?" said Gamma Brooks, leading the way home with a firm step and a strange, determined smile on her face.

*　*　*　*　*

But there was a small glitch in the plans of Shelly and Gamma Brooks. There were no more seats available for flights into Chicago for the following day.

That's why Gamma and Shelly had to catch a midnight flight that same evening.

CHAPTER EIGHT

A SURPRISE FOR PALEOJOE

PaleoJoe hated to fly and this trip had begun very badly. When his alarm failed to go off, he almost missed his flight. In his hurry to get to the airport, he had forgotten his suitcase and had only his rucksack with him that, besides his shaving kit and ancient cell phone, contained mostly books. And search though he would through the jungle of scientific debris that was his office, he had been unable to find his tool roll.

He hated not having it, especially on a case like this one. He felt incomplete without it. It was like going to work without your hat. In sudden panic at that thought PaleoJoe checked his rucksack for his hat, found it missing, and then discovered it on his head.

In his plane seat at last, PaleoJoe looked nervously around him. Usually he had Shelly to distract him when he traveled like this. Had it been a mistake, he wondered, to leave her behind?

No, of course not, he scolded himself. Whoever had stolen Dinosaur Sue out from under the noses of The Field Museum security would be no one to fool around with.

The "Fasten Seat Belt" light came on. Determined to distract himself from thinking about the laws of gravity, PaleoJoe buried his nose in his tattered copy of *Dinosaurs of the World* and began reading about the *T. rex.*

It was raining in Chicago when the plane landed. The museum car and driver were waiting for PaleoJoe.

"Shall I help you get your suitcase?" the driver asked. He was a college kid wearing a Bears t-shirt, but he was friendly and trying to help.

"This is it," said PaleoJoe shortly, slinging his

rucksack over his shoulder.

"Right." Was that admiration or pity in his look? PaleoJoe couldn't be sure and decided to ignore it.

It was raining hard as PaleoJoe and the driver ran to the car. PaleoJoe got a little damp in the process.

It was raining very hard when they pulled up at the museum. The driver directed PaleoJoe to the side entrance. PaleoJoe got monstrously, soakingly, soppy wet as he dashed up the museum steps. PaleoJoe was no sprinter. The rain had plenty of time to do its job.

Inside the door he was calmly met by a small figure holding a pink umbrella in one hand and a large fuzzy towel in the other.

"Poor PaleoJoe," said the figure, sympathetically handing him the towel. "An umbrella really would have been a good idea."

With the rain dripping from his beard and running races down the brim of his floppy hat, PaleoJoe wondered why he was surprised.

He took the towel.

"Thank you, Shelly," he said.

"Always be prepared," Shelly lectured, twirling her pink umbrella. She was wearing pink rain boots to match. "And speaking of being prepared, I thought you would want this."

From her pink backpack Shelly produced PaleoJoe's canvas tool roll.

Wordlessly, PaleoJoe took it from her because, really, what was there to say?

"Whooohooo!" Shelly crowed. "Let's go kick some robber behind!"

And she danced ahead of him into the museum, a miniature force of nature dressed in pink.

CHAPTER NINE

A DINOSAUR TAKES A WALK AND LEAVES A CLUE

In his office Charles Renfro, the museum director, a short, worried man with a mostly bald head, paced back and forth as he explained things to Paleo-Joe and Shelly.

"You don't know," he said. "It's all too much. The date, the footprints, trying to keep a lid on the publicity. I think I'm going to pop!"

Shelly thought he might, too, if his face got much redder.

"What about the date?" she asked.

"October 4th," Renfro said gloomily. "You remember, PaleoJoe. You were there."

"Where?" Shelly demanded.

"At the auction," said PaleoJoe. "The museum bought Sue for over $8 million on October 4th, 1997."

"And the dinosaur was stolen on October 4th," said Shelly, putting it together.

"Right," groaned Renfro. "We really don't know how it happened. We closed for the weekend in order to upgrade some of our security systems and when we came back–disaster!"

"Not a very good security system then," observed Shelly.

"No," sighed Mr. Renfro. "They came highly recommended. But they had to disconnect some of our systems in order to install the newer things. The theft must have taken place in that time."

"Who is the security company?" asked Paleo-Joe.

"They are called Red Alert Security."

"Well," said PaleoJoe, "you'd better show us

the scene of the crime."

Renfro quickly ushered PaleoJoe to the main gallery room. Next to the entry doors stood two big security guards. PaleoJoe thought they looked like they ate nails for breakfast.

"A little like barring the barn door after the horses escaped," whispered Shelly.

"Shhhh!" warned PaleoJoe. "Keep your eyes open, Shelly."

"Wilco."

As they entered the room Shelly saw the enormous platform where Sue once stood. There was a covering of dust all over the floor and, sure enough, giant *T. rex* footprints leading away from the platform.

"Look!" Shelly tugged at PaleoJoe's arm.

"I see it," he said. Quickly he fished around in his rucksack and brought out his camera. He took a picture. "Go ahead and look around, Shelly. Let me know what you discover."

"Right." Shelly started to look around. She knew the drill. Don't touch anything. Keep your eyes open. There are always clues.

At one end of the hall Shelly spotted the skeleton of an *Apatosaurus*. She smiled, thinking about

Bob and his last question. There were other skeletons as well, all untouched. From the ceiling a huge *Pterodactyl,* a flying dinosaur, was suspended on almost invisible wires.

Meanwhile, PaleoJoe decided he had to discover how in the world a giant set of dinosaur bones could be taken out of this room. One thing he was sure of, despite the dusty footprints on the floor, they didn't walk out on their own.

He looked around the museum gallery.

"How big are those doors?" he asked Renfro, pointing to two large doors at the far end of the gallery.

"Well, they are big enough to drive a small truck through," said Renfro. "I don't know what their dimensions are exactly. We use them to get the exhibits in and out. Is it important?"

"Could be," mumbled PaleoJoe scribbling notes in a small notebook.

Looking up to the ceiling he noticed a hook almost hidden in the shadows of the rafters. He took a picture of it. And were those holes in the plaster next to the ceiling rafters? Attaching a telephoto lens to his camera, he took a picture of those as well.

"Probably used some sort of block and tackle

to move the skeleton," he mumbled to himself.

As he was examining the platform Shelly came up and tugged his shirt tail.

"Did you find something?" he asked.

"Look," she said, pointing to the floor where he was standing. "What are those?"

"They look like small round balls of molten metal," said PaleoJoe. "And I think that's what they are. Look here, Shelly." He pointed to the iron supports of Sue's platform. "Those have been cut with a welding torch."

Again he took pictures. He had Shelly place a dime on the floor next to some of the molten balls for scale.

"Well," he said, stowing his camera and notebook back in his rucksack, "I think we are finished here."

"Wait," said Shelly. "Look, PaleoJoe. There is some dirt mixed in with the powder on the floor." Shelly, closer to the floor and with sharp eyes, had detected an important clue.

PaleoJoe knelt down with his magnifying glass to look. "Hmmmm..." he said. "That dirt looks familiar. Shelly, let's scoop up some to examine at the lab."

"Right." From her pink backpack Shelly took out a small plastic bag and a small brush. Gently she scooped up some of the dirt and sealed it in the bag which she gave to PaleoJoe.

"So what happened to Sue?" asked Renfro

eagerly as he escorted PaleoJoe and Shelly back to his office.

"She's been stolen," said Shelly helpfully.

"Yes, well, we know that of course," said PaleoJoe glaring at Shelly who completely ignored him. "I think it's obvious that someone came in over that weekend when the security systems were shut off, cut down the skeleton and carted it away. The question is not really how, but who."

"So, who?" asked Mr. Renfro, sounding like an owl.

"Too early to say," said PaleoJoe. "Have you spoken to your employees? Did anyone see anything?"

"Yes, we talked to everyone. No one on staff was here over the weekend when it happened. No one saw anything."

"Did anyone see anybody who looked suspicious hanging around the museum? Any disgruntled employees?"

"No," Renfro sadly shook his head.

"Okay," said PaleoJoe. "We'll take this information back to my lab and sort through some things. In the meantime, I think you had better call the police. They can check out that security company."

Leaving a gloomy Mr. Renfro to deal with calling the police, Shelly and PaleoJoe met up with Gamma Brooks and left the cool interior of the museum. The rain had stopped.

"So, PaleoJoe," chirped Shelly. "What's the next step?"

CHAPTER TEN

SORTING OUT DETAILS

It turned out that the next step was what Paleo-Joe called Sorting Out Details.

"We make a list," he said, "of everything we know."

"Everything?" Shelly said. That could be an awful lot, thought Shelly.

"Well, everything connected to this case," said PaleoJoe.

So Gamma Brooks made them some hot chocolate and they sat at the little table in the hotel room and got to work.

"First, some history," said PaleoJoe. "Shelly,

go ahead and tell me what you know about Sue."

Shelly quickly covered all the facts she and Gamma Brooks had discussed before. PaleoJoe took notes.

"Good," he said. "What else?"

"The bones were discovered in August 1990 in South Dakota. Sue was the largest and most complete *T. rex* skeleton ever found," Shelly sounded like a professor. "It was significant that they found so many bones in one place."

"Right," PaleoJoe stopped to stroke his beard. "It was a painstaking job to excavate, remove, and clean all those bones so the paleontologists could study them."

Shelly's eyes sparkled. "Can you imagine? It would have been better than finding gold!"

PaleoJoe agreed. "And it was an accident that they found Sue at all!"

It was always an exciting moment when those kinds of fossils were found. And the crew finding Sue had been extraordinarily lucky. So many things could scatter the bones of the ancient dinosaurs—scavengers who ate them, and the action of water, like a river—were just a couple.

"You can almost picture it," said PaleoJoe.

"There they were..."

"There who were?" Shelly interrupted.

"Oh, right. Forgot to be specific, didn't I?" PaleoJoe looked sheepish. "What I meant to say," he continued, "is that there they were, the people of the Black Hills Institute."

"Who are they?" asked Shelly

"A group of dedicated professional and amateur paleontologists who like to look for, discover, and study fossils."

"Man, they sure hit the jackpot that time," said Shelly.

"As I was saying," said PaleoJoe. "There they were just hiking along, prospecting for bones, and then they saw it. It was just a small amount of bone material, weathering out of a cliff about fifty feet tall. The bones were about twenty-one feet from the bottom of the cliff. Ancient bones of the world's largest and most complete *Tyrannosaurus Rex*, just weathering out in the hills and cliffs of the badlands."

"Hey, maybe that's where we should look for our bad guy–in the badlands! Get it?" Shelly laughed.

"Right," PaleoJoe had to scowl to keep from laughing. It wasn't smart to encourage her. "The badlands are those parts of the United States and Canada that were once lush tropical and subtropical areas where dinosaurs once roamed. Now they are bleak, dreary, hot desert areas with little water and little vegetation."

"Just the sort of spot one would want to build a fancy retirement condo!" Shelly laughed.

"Okay, let's focus here," said PaleoJoe. "There was controversy over the find."

"I didn't know about that!" Shelly exclaimed.

"It wasn't a happy event. And it was hard work. First, they had to clear away the dirt and rocks and sediment—what they call the overburden—lying above the layer that contains the bones. When that was accomplished, they wrapped the bones in a protective jacket of plaster almost like you do with a broken arm. The bones could then be safely transported back to the lab."

"Where does the controversy come in?" asked Shelly.

"Well, after they got the bones to the lab, the federal government seized the skeleton and lawsuits began over the ownership of Sue."

PaleoJoe and Shelly thought for a moment.

"Wasn't the skeleton over forty feet long?"

asked Shelly.

"Forty-two feet," said PaleoJoe, recording the fact. "That translates to 12.8 meters on the metric scale."

"That's a lot of skeleton to steal," Shelly observed.

"That's why I think it's important not to forget about that security company that was working at the museum that weekend."

"What were they called again?"

PaleoJoe consulted his notes. "Red Alert Security."

"One thing I don't understand," said Shelly.

"Just one?"

"Seriously."

"Okay. What don't you understand?"

"I don't understand about those footprints. What do you think they are, PaleoJoe?"

"I've thought about that," PaleoJoe admitted. "And what I'm thinking is that whoever has taken Sue is someone with a huge ego—someone who thinks very highly of himself."

"Or herself. It could be a woman," Shelly pointed out.

"In any case, I think the footprints are just sort

59

of a calling card. You know, something for dramatic effect."

"So, what do we have then?" asked Shelly.

PaleoJoe flipped through the notes they just made, scratched his head, and put his pencil behind his ear.

"A missing dinosaur," he said.

CHAPTER ELEVEN

TRILOBITE
INTERRUPTION

Monday at school went fairly fast for Shelly. It was somewhere in the middle of math when she realized that in their discussion she and PaleoJoe had neglected an important piece of the story. After that she could barely wait for the end of the day when she could race to the museum to see PaleoJoe.

She found him as usual in the Tombs, carefully studying the photographs he had taken.

"PaleoJoe!" Shelly burst out with her thought. "Remember the auction of Sue?"

"*Stegosaurus* spikes!" exclaimed PaleoJoe. "We left that out of our discussion didn't we?"

"Yep!" Shelly pulled up her stool and PaleoJoe got out the notebook. "Better go over it now."

"Okay," said PaleoJoe, settling himself. His eyes went unfocused as he thought back. "I was there, just out of curiosity. It was, as we said, on October 4th, 1997. People were very intense that day. There was a lot of yelling and hollering out of bids—I remember that well! You know, some people had those paddles—the kind they flash up when they want to bid—"

"And some people tug their ears," said Shelly. "I saw it on TV once."

"Possibly. I just remember that the bidding was fast and furious. Some people were getting mad as the bidding climbed higher."

Just then they were interrupted by a knock on the door.

"I wonder who that could be?" said PaleoJoe.

Without waiting for an invitation, the door burst open and several people marched into the room, a few of whom were unmistakably police officers.

PaleoJoe remained calm. Shelly began a bit of a jittery dance and fell off her stool, causing it to

crash to the ground and making the police officers jump.

"What can we do for you?" inquired PaleoJoe.

"PaleoJoe?" A man stepped forward. He was short and fat and smelled like garlic. "I'm Detective Franks."

"How can I help you?" asked PaleoJoe.

"You can help me by telling me where you were on the night of October 4th."

"That's the night Sue was stolen," Shelly squeaked from behind PaleoJoe's desk where she was watched the intruders with wide eyes. Did they think PaleoJoe had something to do with the theft?

"Calm down, Shelly," said PaleoJoe. "I was right here preparing a *Stegosaurus* skull."

"Mind if we have a look around?" asked Detective Franks.

"Yes, actually I do," said PaleoJoe. "There are a lot of valuable and fragile things here that could get broken if they are mishandled."

"Like dinosaur bones?" said Franks looking slyly at PaleoJoe.

"Of course dinosaur bones, you trilobite," said Shelly, emerging from behind the desk. "PaleoJoe is a paleontologist!"

"Easy, Shelly," warned PaleoJoe.

But it wasn't really any use. Shelly had gotten indignant.

"If you're here investigating the disappearance of Sue, then you had better get out of the Tombs and get on the job."

"What do you know about the missing dinosaur?" Detective Franks turned his smelly attention to Shelly.

"I know quite a lot, and probably more than you do!" Shelly declared.

"Careful, Shelly," warned PaleoJoe.

"And anyway, what do you expect to accomplish by barging in here and disrupting a perfectly normal scientist at his work?"

"What work, Missy?" Detective Franks was nose to nose with Shelly now. And this was no exaggeration as the short detective was actually almost the same height as Shelly.

"He's studying fossils, you antbrain. And my name is Shelly, not Missy!"

"Shelly, don't insult the nice detective," PaleoJoe said.

"I'm not a nice detective," growled Franks.

"That's what I was afraid of," murmured PaleoJoe.

"Come on, Franks," one of the other policemen said. "We can't do anything here without a warrant anyway."

"That's right!" said Shelly, suddenly remembering her lawyer knowledge—what little there was.

65

"You can't come in here without one of those thingy jiggies and since you don't have one—there's the door, gentlemen!"

Grandly she swept open the door to reveal Bob standing just outside looking mean enough to wrestle alligators. "Our maintenance chief will see you out."

"This way, gents," Bob said with a low growl in his voice.

"We're going," said Franks. "But remember this, PaleoJoe, if you are hiding anything, we'll find out about it."

Detective Franks stomped out the door and the others followed. Shelly slammed the door behind them making the old frosted glass shiver.

There was a moment of silence.

"Trilobite?" PaleoJoe began to laugh. "You called that detective a trilobite?"

"He probably doesn't even have a clue!" said Shelly as she, too, began to laugh.

A few minutes later when Bob returned to check on PaleoJoe and Shelly he found them both laughing so hard tears were streaming down their faces.

CHAPTER TWELVE

A SPECIAL INVITATION

Trilobites were prehistoric sea animals which lived during the Paleozoic Era. They were one of PaleoJoe's favorite fossils. Shelly hadn't meant to insult the trilobite by calling Detective Franks one, but she thought the comparison very funny and was still laughing over it when she told Gamma Brooks about it later.

"Shelly, you little stingbee," said Gamma Brooks, her eyes sparkling. "PaleoJoe is lucky to have you to defend him."

"Well," said Shelly. "He probably didn't really need defending. I just got carried away."

"Well, I know that you are a help to him, anyway," said Gamma Brooks and gave Shelly a hug.

Shelly did not see PaleoJoe for several days after the incident with Detective Franks. She had commitments to some after school activities such as her piano lessons, French lessons, and dance class, but late each night she got out her notebook and went over the details as she knew them, trying to reason out some angle they had not yet considered.

Towards the end of the week Shelly again found time to visit the Balboa after school.

The day had been chilly and the air was full of swirling leaves as Shelly left the school yard that afternoon. Overhead, V-shaped formations of geese cut across the blue of the sky. Shelly was wearing a blue pullover and a sky blue knitted cap with a tassel that bobbed off the top. She was making it spin in interesting ways as she entered the museum.

"Hey, Shelly!" Annie called to her from the reception desk.

Shelly skipped over, enjoying the manic bounce of her tassel on her shoulders. "Hi, Annie!"

"Cute hat," Anne smiled her flash of solar brilliance.

"Thanks," said Shelly, pleased.

"Hey, Shelly. This paper just came in and I know that PaleoJoe will want to see it right away. This letter also came for him. Could you take it all down to the Tombs for me?"

"Sure thing, Annie," said Shelly, taking the items and twirling away.

But when she got to the staircase, Shelly slowed down as she read the banner of the newspaper. It said:

What was this? Shelly's heart began to beat fast. She careened down the stairs and when Bob met her at the closed door of the Tombs she brushed past him with a desperate apology for not playing the game.

"It's an emergency!" she called back over her shoulder. "PaleoJoe's gonna wanna know right now!!"

"PaleoJoe is gonna wanna know what right now?" grumped PaleoJoe as Shelly careened into his office. He had heard her yell all the way down the hall. "In fact," he added, "you might want to go yell that again because I think someone in Australia didn't hear you."

"Sorry," said Shelly. "But look at this, Paleo-Joe. Look! Just look at this paper!"

"I will if you stop flailing it around like raptor bait and give it to me."

"Sorry." Shelly handed over the paper.

"Pish," said PaleoJoe. He fumbled in his shirt pocket for his reading glasses and then found them perched on his head. Settling them in place he began to read:

IP - Germany

Officials at the German National Museum announced today that they will unveil a new *Tyrannosaurus Rex* exhibition next week in the main exhibit hall. The fossil remains of this giant animal of the past may be the biggest *T. rex* ever discovered..."

PaleoJoe's voice trailed off.

"Could it be Sue?" Shelly asked softly.

"I don't know. It says here that they found it three years ago."

"It could be a lie."

"We shouldn't jump to conclusions, Shelly."

"No, but we should go and see for ourselves, don't you think?"

"Maybe," PaleoJoe stroked his beard as he re-read the article.

"Oh," said Shelly. "Here, I almost ˙forgot. Annie said this came for you." She handed him the letter.

It was a strange letter. It was large and square and had a lot of fancy gold writing on it that Shelly couldn't read.

"I don't believe it!" exclaimed PaleoJoe.

"What is it?" Shelly demanded.

"It's an invitation, Shelly."

"Like from who, the Queen? Get a grip PaleoJoe—a party's a party."

"Not this one, Shelly Brooks!" Was PaleoJoe whooping? "This is an invitation from the German National Museum to be present at…"

"The unveiling of the dinosaur!?!" Shelly shrieked.

PaleoJoe nodded eagerly. "And this time, Miss Shelly Brooks, you are going to go with me!"

"Oh yeah!" Shelly invented a new dance step on the spot and hit PaleoJoe in the eye with her flying tassel.

CHAPTER THIRTEEN

PALEOJOE TAKES CHARGE

PaleoJoe made all the arrangements. First, he talked to Gamma Brooks and got her to agree to be a chaperone for Shelly. And if you thought that was hard, then you haven't been paying attention to this story.

Next he tackled Shelly's parents. As a future paleontologist a trip to the German National Museum was a definite priority, he told them. They agreed.

Miss Applewhite, Shelly's teacher, came next and PaleoJoe brushed off his hat and went to see her in person.

73

"If Shelly could miss a week of school," he said, "I will come and give a dinosaur presentation to your class and Shelly will help me."

Who would turn down an offer like that?

And so the plans were made, bags were packed, and Shelly was allowed to pack both her pink backpack and PaleoJoe's rucksack without interference. She was so excited that she thought she would pop just as Mr. Renfro had worried would happen to him.

The day before they were to leave, PaleoJoe received another visit from Detective Franks. Suspicious that PaleoJoe was planning to leave the country, Franks wanted to have another talk with him.

This time Shelly was not present. Maybe that made the conversation easier.

"Did you find anything interesting when you investigated that security company?" PaleoJoe wanted to know.

"No. They seem to be legitimate. They are run by a board of directors, but of course a single person could still be in charge. We're still investigating."

When they parted Detective Franks was less suspicious and PaleoJoe's anxiety that the German *T. rex* could be Sue had increased.

"You'll let me know what you find?" Detective Franks asked.

"Absolutely," PaleoJoe promised.

He meant it too.

On the plane Shelly went into overdrive which annoyed several passengers sitting close by, but for which PaleoJoe was extremely grateful. Flying over

the ocean was a whole lot different than a short hop over Lake Michigan. He hated the thought of both.

"So, PaleoJoe," said Shelly when they were airborne and she had tired of describing clouds to him, "tell me something that I really want to know."

"Okay," said PaleoJoe. "What do you want to know?"

"Why do you carry that ratty old dinosaur book around with you everywhere you go? You know all that stuff, don't you?"

"You mean this ratty old book?" He happened to have it in his lap with his finger marking the place where he had been reading when Shelly had gone into her cloud monologue.

"Yeah, that one."

PaleoJoe carefully opened the book to the inside of the front cover. "There are many reasons," he said. "First, I love this design on the end papers."

Shelly studied the picture—she had never really noticed the drawings before. In a strange green color, the illustration was of an imagined Jurassic landscape that was less scientifically and more imaginatively drawn.

"Can't you imagine standing under one of those trees?" PaleoJoe's voice was soft. "Soon a

Triceratops leaves the safety of the wooded shoreline along a shallow lakeshore. See. There he is. He is hungry and wants to eat some of the soft, lush new fern growth there by the water's edge."

"But over here," Shelly took up the story, pointing at another dinosaur in the illustration, "is a *T. rex* and he is hungry too. Does the *Triceratops* hear his approach? His footsteps must sound like thunder and shake the ground."

"But *Triceratops* is not without defense," adds PaleoJoe. "He will defend himself to the death if necessary."

"Meanwhile, in the deeper lagoon, *Plesiosaur* swims with his long neck straight out looking for the smaller sea creatures that will be his supper."

"That's right," said PaleoJoe.

"Okay, what else about this book?" asked Shelly.

"Well, here is something interesting about it," PaleoJoe flipped to the first page. "See here. What does it say?"

"There's a date," said Shelly, squinting at the small curly type. "It says 1928. Wow, it's an old book too. But PaleoJoe, there have been so many new discoveries since this was written."

"What else does it say?"

"It says 'First Edition.' What does that mean?"

"That means that this edition, which might have been one of several hundreds that were made, was the first printing of this book. That makes it valuable."

"Oh," said Shelly. "So it's valuable and has cool pictures. What else?"

"Okay," said PaleoJoe. "I'll tell you the secret. Look."

He opened the book to the title page. There someone had written something in ink which had faded over time. Shelly had to take the book from PaleoJoe and hold it almost to her nose to read it.

For Joseph,
Who dreams of dinosaurs.
Happy Birthday
Love, Aunt Marie

"So your Aunt Marie gave this to you?"

"No, Shelly. Just how old do you think I am anyway? Don't answer that! My Great great Aunt Marie gave this book to my Grandfather who wanted to study dinosaurs when he was a boy. Don't you see, Shelly? This is a book of dreams."

And for several hours after that Shelly quietly read PaleoJoe's book, learning and dreaming all at the same time.

CHAPTER FOURTEEN

EUROPE BRACES FOR SHELLY

Hotel check-in, a meal, and a nap and Shelly was more than ready to go. The three hailed a cab and headed for the museum.

Gamma Brooks took off for the entomology wing and PaleoJoe and Shelly headed for Dinosaur Hall.

"Did you know that the *Quetzalcoatlus* was the largest flying dinosaur and was about the size of a World War II fighter plane?" Shelly asked PaleoJoe as they made their way through the crowds at the museum.

"Did you read that out of my book?" asked PaleoJoe.

"Of course not," Shelly smirked. "Your book was written before World War II so how would anyone have known that?"

"Smart girl."

The Hall of Dinosaurs was dark and gloomy and BIG. Shelly identified many of her favorite dinosaurs including an *Apatosaurus*, a *Triceratops*, and a *Stegosaurus*. Windows set high on the vaulted walls let in light, and the dinosaurs cast eerie pools of shadow on the dark shiny floor.

Some of the dinosaur skeletons were mounted as Sue had been, freestanding and on platforms. Other dinosaurs were mounted flat on the walls looking as if they were still locked in the sediments in which they had been found. Some were as huge as small houses. Some were as small as ostriches. Some stood on two back legs, some stood on all four.

Shelly loved the *Stegosaurus* with spikes on its tail and the huge plates of his back hunching high in the air. Some of the skeletons were dark brown, like the strong tea Gamma Brooks liked to make, and some were a tarry black.

"Can I take pictures?" asked Shelly producing

three different kinds of cameras from her backpack. She had a small digital camera, her regular 35 mm Pentax with the telephoto lens of which she was an expert, and a disposable camera in a bright yellow jacket that assured its owner it was waterproof–up to a point.

"I'm sure you can," said PaleoJoe. "Just don't get carried away."

"Hey, no prob!" exclaimed Shelly, promptly getting carried away.

She made PaleoJoe stand in front of a huge Woolly Mammoth and pretend as though he were talking to it. She got down on her stomach for a close-up shot of the foot of a *Diplodocus*. She zoomed in on a feather in the hat of a young woman clear across the gallery just because she could, and she acciden-tally took a picture of her own tennis shoe as she was switching around cameras.

Eventually PaleoJoe and Shelly made their way to the center of the hall where a large black cloth was draped over a huge shape. Surrounding it were several armed guards who looked as though they had no sense of humor at all.

Shelly gulped and stood close to PaleoJoe, quickly trying to hide her camera equipment. She

didn't want anyone to think she was taking pictures for any nefarious purposes. (Nefarious was a cool word Bob had taught her. It meant wicked.)

"Guess that must be it," she said.

"Looks like it," agreed PaleoJoe. He looked at

his watch. "We still have a couple of hours before the unveiling. What would you like to do?"

"Let's just look around," said Shelly. "You can tell me about stuff. I can take pictures and collect brochures."

So that's what they did. PaleoJoe had been to Germany before. He spoke the language well, having served in the U.S. Army in Germany for a number of years. He told Shelly how he had come back to Germany to dig fossils in the famous Solnhofen limestone beds.

"Solnhofen is in Bavaria," he explained. "The limestone in the Solnhofen area is a fine-grained yellowish Upper Jurassic limestone. Roman invaders quarried it for the floors of their baths."

"Gosh," said Shelly, impressed. She was imagining a yellow stone floor in her bathroom at home instead of the blue and white checkered tile her mother had chosen.

In one display case PaleoJoe found a very interesting dinosaur.

"Look, Shelly! What do you think about that?"

Shelly looked and saw what looked like a drawing on a piece of stone. It wasn't a picture though, it was a fossil. In sharp detail she could see every part of the small elegant creature etched there. It had strong hind legs, a long tail, and smaller forelimbs with claw tipped hands, a long neck bent backwards connected to a delicately boned skull. But the most surprising thing of all was the much tinier skeleton of a lizard which could be seen among its ribs. Dinner.

"What is it?" asked Shelly.

"*Compsognathus*," said PaleoJoe. "It means 'elegant jaw.' It was first found in the Solnhofen area in the late 1850's by a man named Oberndorfer. Now, Shelly, look at this next dinosaur."

In the case next to the *Compsognathus* was another skeleton about the size of a crow that Shelly recognized at once.

"That's an *Archaeopteryx*."

"Right," said PaleoJoe. "*Archaeopteryx* means 'ancient wing.' Do you see the similarity to *Compsognathus*?"

Shelly pressed her face closer to the glass in order to see better. The bird's skeleton was made of heavy bones that looked like those of a reptile, but it also had short wings which ended in three clawed fingers.

"Yes," said Shelly. "In fact, if the

Archaeopteryx did not have wings it would look just like a reptile."

"You are looking at what some scientists argue is the link between reptiles and birds. *Archaeopteryx* and *Compsognathus* are like stepping stones between the two species."

"Wow," Shelly's breath fogged the display window.

"Okay," said PaleoJoe. "I think it's about time to go back."

"Do you think this dinosaur is Sue?" asked Shelly anxiously.

"There is no way to know until we see it," answered PaleoJoe.

CHAPTER FIFTEEN

VIP
VERY IMPORTANT
PALEONTOLOGISTS

Shelly and PaleoJoe made their way back to the main exhibition hall and the hidden figure under the black cloth. A large crowd had gathered. From his pocket PaleoJoe produced his invitation.

"Come on, Shelly," he said. "We're VIP, so we can get up in front."

"What's VIP?" asked Shelly. "Very Important Paleontologists?"

87

PaleoJoe laughed. "It should be!" he said. "It means Very Important Person–just that we've been specially invited."

"Right."

They made their way to the front. As they passed a group of people, PaleoJoe frowned.

"Shelly," he put a hand on her arm. "Do you see that man standing there at the edge of that group of people? The short guy?"

Shelly stood on tiptoe to get a view. "You mean the one wearing the hat that looks like a green dinner plate?

"Yes. Do you recognize him?"

"No. Why do you suppose he squints like that? Think he has something in his eye?"

"Never mind. Don't stare!"

"Sorry."

They pushed and smunched and jostled their way to the front of the crowd. PaleoJoe presented his invitation to a tall elegant woman standing beside a section of roped off chairs and they were shown to a couple of seats in the very front. A man got up behind a microphone and began to speak. PaleoJoe began to fidget. He twisted his hat in his hands, he crumpled the program in his fist, and when he started tapping his foot Shelly elbowed him the ribs.

"Sit still, can't you?" she complained.

"Pish!" grumbled PaleoJoe, but did his best.

The man behind the microphone rambled on about the scientists who had discovered the dinosaur that was about to be unveiled.

"And while we are not at liberty to tell you exactly where these bones were discovered..." he said.

"*Pterodactyl* wings!" PaleoJoe snorted.

"What is it?" asked Shelly.

"Oh, nothing," PaleoJoe answered, beginning his hat twirl again. "It's just that if we knew where the bones were found we could tell a lot more about them. You see, modern science has allowed the paleontologist to recreate the lifestyle of some dinosaurs by reading the evidence surrounding the skeleton and the skeleton itself. By the other plants and animals found buried alongside the prehistoric giants, we can determine what life was like long ago."

"You mean things like Sue's broken ribs," said Shelly.

"Yep, things like that," agreed PaleoJoe.

The skeleton of Sue had sustained an injury to three of her ribs. Sometime during her life they had been broken and had begun to heal. Scientists had also determined that Sue had suffered from an infection which made the bones grow back together with a spongy bone growth between them called a callus. The growth showed that the dinosaur lived a long time after the original injury.

"Okay," said PaleoJoe. "Here we go!"

He and Shelly slid forward to the edge of their seats as the guards surrounding the exhibit took up positions around the edges of the black cloth. At a sign from the man behind the microphone, they pulled slender ropes and the cloth lifted like a veil to reveal the dinosaur skeleton underneath.

PaleoJoe was leaning so far forward in his seat that as applause exploded around the room he fell off. No one but Shelly and a large red-faced lady sitting next to him noticed.

"Are you okay?" Shelly tried not to laugh, but it was awful hard.

"I'm fine," said PaleoJoe, grumpily brushing off his pants.

Together he and Shelly stood along with the crowd and applauded the new exhibit, only Shelly and PaleoJoe were not applauding as enthusiastically as everyone else.

The new German *T. rex* was not Sue.

No broken ribs.

"Well," sighed Shelly. "I guess in one way it's a good thing."

"But in another it's quite bad," said PaleoJoe. "Back to work, Shelly."

CHAPTER SIXTEEN

SMUGGLERS

Shelly and PaleoJoe gave their dinosaur presentation to Shelly's class when they returned from their trip. Shelly told the story about the *Archaeopteryx* and the *Compsognathus*. She showed all her pictures including the one of the feather and her shoe and displayed all of her brochures.

PaleoJoe was a big hit with his examples of fossils and his talk about *T. rexes*.

The presentation had been at the end of the day so Shelly was able to walk with PaleoJoe to the museum after school.

"So, what now, PaleoJoe?" Shelly asked.

"How are we going to find Sue?"

PaleoJoe stroked his beard and looked thoughtful. "I don't know. We'll have to do some hard thinking."

When they got to PaleoJoe's office in the Tombs they were surprised to see Detective Franks waiting for them.

"Be polite," PaleoJoe hissed at Shelly before she even had time to realize who their visitor was.

"Need to talk to you, PaleoJoe," Detective Franks said. "You can run along little girl. This is grown-up talk."

"Je desire une pomme," said Shelly with a great deal of insulted royal highness in her tone and walked out, carefully closing the door behind her.

"Huh?" Detective Franks looked completely lost.

"French," PaleoJoe explained. "She said she wanted an apple."

"I see," said Detective Franks clearly not seeing at all. "But, look, PaleoJoe—we could use your help down at U.S. Customs."

"What's up?"

"The Customs fellows intercepted a shipment of some large dinosaur bones. We're concerned about black market fossils, of course."

"Hmmm," said PaleoJoe. "Sounds nefarious."

Shelly, who was as you have probably guessed, listening at the door, suppressed a giggle. She loved that word!

"Well, we'd like it if you would come down and check it out."

"No problem. But I will need to take my assistant along."

"Of course," said Detective Franks politely, never in the least suspecting what that meant.

On the ride down to the Customs office Shelly tried to be as annoying as possible purely for the sake of Detective Franks, or "du concombre" as she was now fondly calling him. Detective Franks had no clue that "du concombre" meant "some cucumber" in French and that Shelly was making a nefarious remark about his physique.

"Is this really a police car? Because it doesn't look like a police car," said Shelly. "In fact, I have never seen a purple police car in my life."

"It's maroon," Detective Franks informed her. Maroon happened to be one of his favorite colors.

"Of course it is, du concombre," said Shelly

sympathetically. "Only some people would mistake it for purple and might not believe that you are a police officer at all. Only I guess you aren't, are you? You're a detective. And a detective isn't really a police officer, is he?"

"When you said assistant," growled Detective Franks to PaleoJoe, "I did not think you meant menace."

PaleoJoe had to turn his head and look out the window so Detective Franks wouldn't see him smile.

Shelly started to sing.

Maybe it was because Detective Franks was driving faster than usual that it did not take any time at all to reach the Customs building where they were holding the crates in question.

Inside they met Lieutenant Richard Boatman, a young man with a short blond crew cut and a big white smile in a very tanned face. Shelly liked him, especially after he winked at her when PaleoJoe introduced her as his assistant.

"It's smart to have an extra pair of sharp eyes," Lt. Boatman said.

"What made you question these crates?" asked PaleoJoe as Lt. Boatman guided them to the area

96

where they had impounded the crates.

"Well, you know we are always on the alert for smugglers," he said.

"Smugglers!" exclaimed Shelly. "You mean like pirates?"

"Modern day pirates, of a sort," Lt. Boatman agreed. "There is a pretty big market for stolen fossils. Most of the stuff comes out of China, Morocco, and Europe, but there are some 'pirates' who are smuggling fossils out of the United States too."

"It's a problem," said PaleoJoe. "There are collectors all over the world who would love to get a real dinosaur bone."

"There are laws protecting vertebrate fossil finds because of their importance," said Detective Franks. He wanted them to know that he wasn't completely lost in the conversation.

"What does that mean?" asked Shelly, and even though the question made Detective Franks smirk she was glad she asked because she really didn't know.

"Paleontologists, as well as the government, know the value of vertebrate bone material," PaleoJoe explained. "Marine invertebrates—you know, sea animals without backbones, plants, and other small fossils—"

"Like the crinoids," said Shelly.

"Right. Like the crinoids. Those kinds of fossils are so common that anyone can easily pick them up without destroying science of the fossil record."

"Fossilized vertebrate bones are another story," said Lt. Boatman. "Franks, give me a hand getting this thing open, will you?"

Crowbars in hand, the two men began to pry open the top of a large crate.

"Detective Franks here put us on the alert after Sue went missing, so when these crates came through and we saw they contained bones we thought someone had better take a look."

With a loud crack and crash the top came loose and tumbled to the ground. Detective Franks skipped out of the way just in time to avoid becoming *du* flat *concombre*.

Lt. Boatman pulled out handfuls of white and pink packing peanuts. PaleoJoe peered into the crate. He could see bones. Big bones.

"What are they?" asked Shelly, just barely able to peer over the side of the box.

"Big bones," said Detective Franks.

"They are mammoth leg bones," identified PaleoJoe.

"That's what I said," gruffed Detective Franks. "Really big bones."

"No, mammoth as in Woolly Mammoth, *du concombre*," explained Shelly.

Lt. Boatman, who actually spoke French, looked a little startled and then began to laugh.

"So not what we are looking for?" Detective Franks was disappointed.

"Not what we are looking for," said PaleoJoe.

CHAPTER SEVENTEEN

A CLUE EXPLAINED

After all, dirt is not just dirt.

That's what PaleoJoe was thinking as Shelly handed him the little plastic bag of dirt that she had collected at the scene of the crime.

"You really think this could be something?" Shelly asked.

"I don't know," said PaleoJoe. "But it's a clue that you gathered up that we haven't really investigated. Dirt has many different properties. It can have a high concentration of sand grains or traces of volcanic ash or even the remains of organic matter, like plant spores. Because of its composition, dirt can actually be traced back to its area of origin."

"It depends on where you get it from, then," said Shelly.

"That's right."

"So this dirt could have come off the bad guy's boot or maybe from Sue herself when she walked out of the museum."

"Very funny."

"Well, I wouldn't blame her if she did. Dinosaurs should have rights too, you know. Maybe she wanted a bigger salary and better benefits."

"Let's look at this beneath the stereomicroscope," suggested PaleoJoe, ignoring Shelly's attempt at humor. Sometimes that was best.

Shelly carefully prepared the slide for PaleoJoe. She knew exactly how to do it and her smaller fingers and steadier hand could get the job done faster.

PaleoJoe pushed his glasses up on his head — he had to use them as he watched Shelly prepare the slide — and peered through the eyepiece. Carefully he made some adjustments.

Then for a really long time he got very still as he stared at the dirt.

A really long time.

An incredibly long time.

After three minutes Shelly got impatient.

"Let me see!"

PaleoJoe backed away and Shelly stood on tiptoe to look. Magnified, the dirt looked like large chunks of rock or crystal.

"Hmmmm…" she said. "Very interesting, indeed."

"What is?" asked PaleoJoe.

"I don't know," Shelly confessed. "I'm sorry, PaleoJoe, but it just looks like giant chunks of dirt to me."

PaleoJoe put his eye back to the scope. "Yeah," he agreed. "To me too, but you know what, Shelly? It's familiar chunks of giant dirt."

"What do you mean?"

"I mean I've seen this dirt before. I think it's dirt from South Dakota."

"And that IS very interesting," said Shelly, "because that's where Sue was found."

"Exactly."

"It couldn't have come from the bones because they would have been very clean."

"Right," said PaleoJoe still looking at the dirt. "No matrix remains after the scientists clean the bones."

"What's matrix?" asked Shelly.

"Matrix is the rock material the bone was

found in. Sometimes it is very hard and sometimes soft. In any case, it has to be removed so the bones can be preserved."

"You know, PaleoJoe, whoever stole Sue would have had to put the bones in something to cart them off. They would have been too heavy to just carry."

"That's true," PaleoJoe sat back looking thoughtful and stroking his beard.

"So maybe that dirt came off of tires or something. Maybe from some sort of cart that whoever used to steal Sue."

"Or something," agreed PaleoJoe. "Let's take another look at those photos I took."

Quickly Shelly dug them out of a drawer.

"Look!" exclaimed PaleoJoe. "Just what I remembered seeing. See all those small holes in the ceiling?"

"Do you think it was a maniac woodpecker?" Shelly chuckled. "Sorry," she apologized, seeing the scowl on PaleoJoe's face. "I know what you think. You think someone shot something at the ceiling and had bad aim."

"Yes, I do. They had to make some sort of rope and pulley system to haul the bones into whatever they brought in."

"Which was the thing leaving dirt on the floor!" exclaimed Shelly in triumph.

"Yes," agreed PaleoJoe. "Whatever it was."

CHAPTER EIGHTEEN

AUCTION LOSERS

Two days later the case blew wide open. This is how it happened.

Shelly was sitting in PaleoJoe's office entertaining herself because PaleoJoe was in one of his don't-bother-me-I'm-trying-to-think moods. She was sitting, or twirling rather, on PaleoJoe's swivel chair, a chair Shelly dearly loved and would have liked to have for her very own.

She was playing a game she had seen on TV. Someone would guess something and then the host would say in an impressive voice: "And the winner is..." Shelly had a stack of paper crumpled up into tight balls. She swiveled on the chair and let one of her paper balls fly into the recycle bin on the other side of the room. Whenever she made it into the basket she would spin very fast and crow: "And the winner is du concombre!!"

Very funny.

At least Shelly thought so.

Until one of her crumpled paper balls hit PaleoJoe on the end of his nose.

"SHELLY!!" he roared in a tone of voice that indicated he wasn't too pleased.

"And the winner is PaleoJoe?" Shelly suggested apologetically.

At first PaleoJoe looked like he was going to scold her, but then his face turned sort of pink and it looked like maybe he had swallowed something unexpectedly. His eyes got wide. Suddenly he leaped to his feet.

"SHELLY!! That's it!" He fired the paper at the recycle bin, hit it in one, and tore out the door.
In an instant Shelly was pounding after him.

"Wait! What's it? Where are you going? Slow down!"

But PaleoJoe did not slow down until he burst

107

into Annie's office and just about caused her to faint.

Shelly was impressed. Even she didn't burst into rooms with quite so much ferocity.

"Annie," said PaleoJoe, with as sweet a smile as he could muster. "Work your magic and get me a list of all the people who bid at the auction for dinosaur Sue on October 4th, 1997. Please…"

"No problem," said Annie. "Just don't trash my office while you're in here."

She said that because PaleoJoe in his agitation had just upset a stack of papers on her desk. While Shelly helped him pick up the papers, Annie swiveled to her computer and her fingers flew like swift swallows over the keyboard.

"Okay, PaleoJoe," she said after a few minutes. "A copy of the names will be faxed to me shortly."

"How…?" PaleoJoe was impressed.

"Don't ask," said Annie giving him one of her golden smiles. "It's the old girl secretary network in operation. Sometimes I think we might be better than the FBI. Also, do you want a copy of the video tape of the auction?"

"Is there such a thing?" asked PaleoJoe. He sounded like someone who had just been told the streets were made of candy delights.

Annie winked. "You betcha!"

Shelly had to help PaleoJoe back to his office. He seemed to be quite distracted.

"What is it!?" she demanded.

"It's everything," said PaleoJoe. "Because I think the person who stole Sue is someone who lost at the auction."

"Oh!" Shelly was impressed. "And the loser is..."

CHAPTER NINETEEN

DUEL AT THE AUCTION

The faxed list of names came within a few minutes. When Shelly finally went home PaleoJoe was still pouring over it trying to recognize names.

Shelly arrived in the Tombs after school the next day to find PaleoJoe's office set up with a TV and VCR and to find Detective Franks sitting in the swivel chair.

"Come on in, Shelly," said PaleoJoe.

"Okay, your assistant is here now," grumped Detective Franks. "Can we get on with it?"

"Shelly, if you would be so good as to get the lights?"

Darkness engulfed the little room. The eerie blue glow of the TV made strange shadows on Detective Franks' round face as he leaned close. PaleoJoe hit the play button on the remote control.

The screen filled with the picture of a large room full of well-dressed people. The camera panned here and there, bringing people in and out of focus. Pictures of Sue were hung all around the richly furnished room. On special easels in the front were large framed pictures and close-ups of the dinosaur fossil that was soon to be auctioned off.

When the auctioneer took his place behind the podium, the camera focused on him and the room began to get silent. He was a round man with a heavy, red face.

"Du concombre!"

Had that come from Detective Franks? Shelly looked at him in surprise and almost fell out of her chair when she saw him actually wink at her!

The auctioneer in his dark suit and blindingly white shirt and bow tie cleared his throat and rapped his auctioneer's gavel on the podium.

Instant silence.

Everyone sat on rich upholstered chairs and waited.

"Now, we will begin the bid for this set of fossil *T. rex* dinosaur bones known as Sue," said the auctioneer, and the bidding began.

It was like watching an exciting football game only the players were invisible and there was no tackling involved. Each bidder had a wooden paddle with a number on it. When someone wanted to raise the bid, they raised their paddle.

Five hundred thousand dollars.

Up went a paddle.

Three and a half million.

Up went another paddle.

Six million.

Fewer and fewer paddles were going up.

Seven million.

A scatter of paddles swatted the air.

Seven million, two hundred thousand dollars.

And now there were only three people left bidding. It was like a duel. PaleoJoe paused the tape.

"Look," he said, pointing to the figures in the fuzzed and jumpy frozen picture. "That man there in the pinstripe suit is Mr. Renfro, The Field Museum director. That woman in the orange dress is a representative for some movie star who wanted Sue to decorate his mansion. And that man there…the one in the red tie wearing that flat, funny looking hat? Keep your eyes on him."

Mr. Renfro signaled with his paddle.

Seven million, six hundred thousand dollars.

There was a pause.

"That's a lot of money," Shelly softly whistled.

"You ain't just a flappin' yer jaw," said Detective Franks, suddenly showing an unexpected sense of humor.

The little man in the red tie and funny hat threw his paddle to the ground and stomped on it.

"Sold!" said the auctioneer, "for $7.6 million!" With taxes and auction premiums, the museum had paid a total of $8.36 million.

PaleoJoe reversed the tape and froze it on the little man as he jumped on his auction paddle.

"I think that's your man," he said.

CHAPTER TWENTY

SHELLY GOES UNDERCOVER

It had to be said, thought Shelly Brooks, that once Detective Franks got hold of the scent of the criminal he was like a bulldog. After viewing the video, Detective Franks and PaleoJoe headed downtown to the police station. Shelly had been invited too—by Detective Franks no less—but had to decline as she had homework waiting for her at home.

Later, PaleoJoe called her and filled her in on all the details.

They had discovered that the man in the funny hat was a private collector of fossils by the name of Sir Franklin J. Higgenbottom. He was an eccentric multimillionaire and he lived in...

"Guess where," said PaleoJoe.

"South Dakota," said Shelly.

"Right. Tomorrow Detective Franks and his team are going to fly out there to do some investigating. I have to go because I can identify Sue if we find her."

"Tomorrow is Saturday," said Shelly as though making a casual observation.

"I did say that I would need my assistant," said PaleoJoe.

So, the next morning, pink backpack slung over her shoulder, Shelly was waiting in her front yard for PaleoJoe to pick her up. They flew with Detective Franks and two of his men aboard a DC-9. The detectives looked just like everybody else and Shelly began to think about how cool it might be to travel undercover like that.

When they landed the detectives rented a van. They headed out.

The Higgenbottom mansion was out in the middle of nowhere. Using a sophisticated GPS

device, Detective Franks had no difficulty in locating it. They drove up a long and winding drive.

The mansion sat back from the driveway under the shade of trees. It had a green sweep of lawn that probably required a lake to keep it growing.

A limestone path studded with fossils led up to the front door.

"Wait a minute," said Shelly pushing ahead. "I can handle this."

"Oh no you don't," said Detective Franks grabbing her shoulder.

"No, seriously," said Shelly, all fooling aside. She was very serious. "You don't have a warrant to search this guy's mansion any more than you did when you came busting into PaleoJoe's office, right?"

Detective Franks looked embarrassed. His two men suddenly found the sky to be a very interesting thing, and became absorbed in observing the clouds.

"Let me go to the door. It'll be like I'm undercover. I'll pretend to be selling cookies or something. You guys just stand by. I can get us in. We have to do this right, Detective Franks."

Franks looked at PaleoJoe.

"She can do it," he said.

"Okay. But no cookies."

"Why not?"

"Where are they?" Detective Franks raised an eyebrow at Shelly.

"Oh. Good point."

"We'll be right here. Be careful." Franks was serious too.

Shelly approached the big front door. Paleo-Joe and the detectives waited not far down the path near a rock garden that was made of giant fossil coral heads.

Shelly rang the doorbell and jumped about a foot in the air! The thing sounded like the roar of a giant...well...dinosaur!

"Cool!" Shelly couldn't help herself. It was cool and now she knew exactly what she was going to say when someone came to the door.

But no one did.

She pushed the bell again and this time kept her finger pushed down.

Rrrrrooooaaarrrrr!!

The door jerked open and Shelly was confronted by a little man dressed in a big floppy hat, a safari coat with lots of pockets, faded old blue jeans, and hiking boots.

Without a doubt, she was face to face with Sir Franklin J. Higgenbottom.

CHAPTER TWENTY-ONE

THE TREASURES OF HIGGENBOTTOM MANSION

"Mr. Higgenbottom?" Shelly ignited her best smile.

The man looked suspiciously at her.

"Aardly," he said.

Shelly almost laughed out loud. Mr. Higgenbottom was trying to disguise his voice with a fake British accent. A bad, fake British accent.

"Master 'Iggenbottom is not at home. I am the butler."

119

"Oh, that's too bad," Shelly pouted. "I came all this way to see some of his famous collection."

"Famous?" the fake butler paused in the act of closing the door on Shelly.

"Oh, yes. You see, I want to be a paleontologist when I grow up and my daddy said there ain't nobody who has a better collection of them fossils then does Mr. Higgenbottom up the hill." Shelly could do different voices. Today she would be undercover as the gushing dumb kid with bad grammar. She was convincing.

Higgenbottom bought it.

"Oh, well, I'm sure the Master wouldn't mind if you came in for a peek. I can show you around myself."

"Could you?" Maybe clapping her hands like that was a bit over the top, but Shelly did it anyway.

"Sure. Sure. Come on in."

The door opened wide.

"He said we could take a look, Daddy!" Shelly squealed and darted inside.

"Daddy?" But before Higgenbottom could really do anything about it both PaleoJoe and Detective Franks were also inside.

"Hey, what's the meaning of this?" the Butler

demanded, letting his accent slip a little.

"Oh, this is my daddy," said Shelly, introducing PaleoJoe. "And this is my cousin Franks. He's mute," she added, grinning wickedly at Detective Franks whose face was getting a reddish tint. "He hasn't said a word since the day he was born. Sad really." And Shelly elbowed him in the side.

"Too bad," said the fake butler with not a single trace of sympathy in his voice. "Please come this way and I'll show you the fossil room. Don't touch anything."

They followed Higgenbottom through a long hallway, through a gold colored door and into a large open area. Bright light shone and sparkled off rows and rows of glass cases. Here and there were dinosaur bones propped on display pedestals and in a far corner there was what looked to be a complete skeleton of a Stegosaurus. It looked like the exhibit hall of a museum.

"*Triceratops* scales!" said PaleoJoe.

"Impressive, isn't it?" Higgenbottom could not resist a gloating smile.

They worked their way down row after row of cases, each filled with fossils. Several times PaleoJoe stopped to stare, astonished at what he was seeing. He began to ask Higgenbottom questions, but captured by the zeal of his passion for fossils, Higgenbottom never noticed how much PaleoJoe actually knew about what he was looking at. And of course Detective Franks, undercover as Shelly's mute cousin, couldn't say a word.

CHAPTER TWENTY-TWO

MYSTERY IN THE SAND

PaleoJoe lured the fake butler, who was really Higgenbottom himself, around the room of fossils. Shelly, trying to ignore the fabulous curiosities on display, hung back trying to discover the clue they were going to need to solve this mystery.

The afternoon sun streamed in through big French doors lighting up the room. As Shelly paused in front of them she happened to glance out. She could see the long sweep of Higgenbottom's emerald green lawn. Fancy flower beds bordered his backyard which eventually gave way to the sandy landscape of the distant hills.

But what was that just on the rim of the horizon?

Shelly turned to motion Detective Franks over. He came to peer over her shoulder.

"It looks like tents," said Shelly.

Just then Higgenbottom approached.

"What are you looking at?" he demanded,

"What's that out there on the hill?" Shelly pointed.

"It looks like tents," said PaleoJoe, squinting against the sunlight.

"Oh, I wouldn't pay any attention to that," said Higgenbottom. "That's just something the neighbors are doing. Now, if I could direct your attention to the fossils over here…"

"What," said PaleoJoe refusing to budge, "exactly are the neighbors doing?"

"Oh, nothing really," Higgenbottom appeared nervous.

"I'd like to take a look," said PaleoJoe.

"It's quite a hike out there," said Higgenbottom. "I'm sure the little girl doesn't want to get all hot and dusty."

"Actually, I like dust," said Shelly, and she pushed open the doors and marched outside with PaleoJoe and Detective Franks close behind.

Higgenbottom groaned, sounding like a man in pain, and followed them.

Higgenbottom had been right about one thing. It was a hot and dusty walk. It took the group about ten minutes to hike out to the hill where Shelly had spotted the tents. Glancing back over her shoulder Shelly caught sight of Detective Franks' men following at a distance. She tried to keep up a steady stream of chatter to distract Higgenbottom so he wouldn't look back and see them.

When they reached the rim of the hill, they could clearly see that the tents were clustered at one end of what looked to be a dig site. Just visible from where they stood were what looked to be large bones

half in and partly out of the sandy and rocky sur-
roundings.

"Well, well," said PaleoJoe. "It looks like the
neighbors have been busy."

CHAPTER TWENTY-THREE

DETECTIVE FRANKS ALWAYS GETS HIS MAN

PaleoJoe took a careful look at this very strange dig site as they entered it. Most dig sites have piles and piles of dirt. There were none here. Many sites are hilly and dinosaur bones weather out of a hill. This ground was nearly flat.

There were bones all right, but they were all laid out and there was no evidence of plaster any-where.

Going up to look at the bones closely, he could see that they were dusty but remarkably complete.

It looked to PaleoJoe as though someone had just buried bones that had already been excavated, cleaned, and prepared.

Shading his eyes against the glare of the afternoon sun, PaleoJoe could see none of the usual tools and equipment that litter the dig sites of most paleontologists. The skeleton itself did not seem to be buried very deep. The little dirt that was on top of the skeleton looked as if it had been recently put there.

"This dig site is fake," PaleoJoe announced.

"I assure you," said the fake butler, "that this is a very real dig site."

"Not the neighbors, then?" asked Shelly.

Higgenbottom gave her a look that Shelly merely smiled at. "No. Not the neighbors. I only said that to keep you away. This is Mr. 'Iggenbottom's personal dig site and you should not be trespassing here."

"Is that how you keep the site secure?" asked PaleoJoe.

"Oh, we're not concerned with security," Higgenbottom sounded like he was bragging. "After all Mr. 'Iggenbottom owns one of the best security firms in the country."

"Which one is that?" asked PaleoJoe. "I've

been thinking about beefing up the security in my lab, you see," he added, trying not to arouse the suspicion of Higgenbottom.

Shelly understood right away why PaleoJoe was asking. The same question had been in her mind.

"He owns Red Alert Security," said Higgenbottom. "I can put you in touch with the sales department, if you would like."

"Thank you." PaleoJoe did a good imitation of someone who had not just been given a significant clue to a mystery.

In fact, Shelly heard Detective Franks give a sort of strangled gargle. But it wasn't time to make a move. Not yet. They had to learn more.

"Have you been documenting this site by drawings and photos?" asked PaleoJoe.

"Of course. Do you think we are amateurs here? This skeleton that you are looking at is the greatest find of the century. You probably don't know what it is you are looking at, but I assure you that this is one of the biggest and most complete *T. rex* skeletons ever found. And I can also assure you, sir, that the whole world will know that I was the one that found it!"

"Mr. Higgenbottom's butler?" Shelly asked doubtfully.

"Okay, okay. So you found me out. I am not the butler, I am really Higgenbottom himself. But who cares! This is the greatest discovery of all time!"

"Well," said Detective Franks, deciding the moment had come and breaking his silence. "Actually, I care. I'm not really a mute cousin." He flashed his ID and Higgenbottom looked a little pale even under the bright afternoon sun. "And I've been looking for you."

"And you might be interested to know that this isn't my daddy," piped up Shelly. "This is really PaleoJoe, the Dinosaur Detective."

And then, all of a sudden, Mr. Higgenbottom had to sit down.

CHAPTER TWENTY-FOUR

PALEOJOE, DINOSAUR DETECTIVE

Detective Franks summoned his two partners and they stood close by while Shelly helped PaleoJoe unpack his tool roll. As he rolled it out, Shelly ran her eyes over the neat rows of tools fastened securely to the cloth in little pockets and loops. Small chisels, dental picks of all sizes, small brushes, diluted glue, chisels, trowels, and even hammers all neatly stowed away in the canvas roll.

"Well," said PaleoJoe, kneeling down by one

of the bones. Shelly, close beside him, watched everything he did. "Just by looking at these bones you are supposedly finding after sixty-five million years, I would say they are too perfect."

"I'm sure you know all about it," Higgenbottom meant for that to sound snotty, but he only sounded scared. PaleoJoe ignored him.

Carefully, PaleoJoe pulled up a leg bone. "The tibia is coming right out of the ground," he said. "There is no resistance."

Moving over to another bone, PaleoJoe selected a brush from his tool roll and handed a second one to Shelly. "Help me expose this bone," he said.

Together they brushed away dirt. Flies buzzed and the sun shone brightly. Detective Franks was sweating. Higgenbottom was sweating more.

"Here, PaleoJoe," said Shelly. "Here's some more bone."

"It looks like the end of a fibula, one of the two lower leg bones. Keep brushing."

PaleoJoe had to stand up to unkink his back. As his shadow fell over the rib bone Shelly was working on, he heard her gasp.

"What is it?" he asked, quickly kneeling beside her.

"PaleoJoe, this is—" Shelly almost couldn't get the words out. "THIS IS SUE!"

"WHAT?" Detective Franks leaped forward. "How do you know?"

"*Iguanodon* gizzards and *Triceratops* horns!" shouted PaleoJoe. "This is Sue, all right. Look here, Franks. I'll show you what Shelly found."

Detective Franks bent down and, out of the surrounding dusty dirt, PaleoJoe traced the damage to the bone and the regrowth of bone tissue that formed a callus.

"No, it's mine!" screamed Higgenbottom.

But it didn't do him any good. One of the detectives produced a pair of handcuffs and the other one started reading Higgenbottom his rights.

Shelly and PaleoJoe stood side by side in the bright sun, grinning down at the old bones of the most famous dinosaur in the world.

CHAPTER TWENTY-FIVE

HOME AGAIN

Things moved very quickly. PaleoJoe used Shelly's cell phone, because he couldn't get reception on his, to call Mr. Renfro and tell him then and there that Sue had been found. Shelly could hear a lot of banging and shouting from the other end, so she thought Mr. Renfro must be quite happy.

Over the next several days, teams of paleontologists and museum technicians were sent to the Higgenbottom site in South Dakota to recover Sue.

A week after all the fuss had died down Shelly was sitting in the Tombs with PaleoJoe when they got a visit from Detective Franks.

After they had invited him in, Detective Franks gave Shelly something that was wrapped neatly in shiny blue paper and had a yellow bow on it.

"It isn't my birthday," said Shelly.

"Well, this isn't a birthday present, either," said Detective Frank. "Don't open it now. You can wait until I leave. I just wanted you to know that charges have been brought against Higgenbottom. The case is tight and he will probably go to jail for a long time."

"Well, he probably deserves it," said PaleoJoe.

"Sue is back in place and the exhibit is open again. The bones were in good shape and there was no damage."

"That's good," said Shelly.

"There is talk of turning the Higgenbottom mansion into a tourist attraction which will feature a fully operational replica dig site."

"Cool," said Shelly. "It was sort of exciting to find those bones buried like that. I can't imagine what it must be like to actually discover the real thing."

"Well, I have no doubt that someday you will find out," said Detective Franks. He shook PaleoJoe by the hand, tossed Shelly a wink, and left closing the door softly behind him.

"One thing is for sure," said Shelly. "I'm really going to enjoy using my reward."

"A lifetime membership pass to The Field Museum is a very lucky thing to have," agreed PaleoJoe. "Are you going to unwrap your gift from Detective Franks?"

"I wonder what it is," said Shelly as she quickly ripped off the bright paper.

It was a book. And it wasn't a new book.

"Ohmigosh!" Shelly gasped. "Look at this, PaleoJoe. It's a first edition! It's a book about a guy named Roland T. Bird. Who was he?"

"He was a famous fossil hunter," said PaleoJoe smiling. "He rode around the United States on his Harley looking for dinosaur fossils and footprints."

Shelly's eyes began to sparkle. She opened the cover of the book. "Look! Detective Franks wrote something."

On the flyleaf in small and careful letters was written:

To Shelly Brooks,
> **Until the Next Adventure!**
> **From,**
>> **Detective Franks**

"A fossil hunter on a Harley motorcycle, you say?" Shelly began to read.

And so there was really no one to see the faraway look in the eyes of PaleoJoe or to see the smile that crept across his face.

Roland T. Bird

The End

About PaleoJoe

PaleoJoe is a real paleontologist whose recent adventures included digging in the famous Como Bluff for *Allosaurus, Camptosaurus,* and *Apatosaurus.*

A graduate of Niagara University just outside of the fossil rich Niagara Falls and Lewiston area of New York, Joseph has collected fossils since he was 10 years old. He has gone on digs around the United States and abroad, hunting for dinosaur fossils with some of the most famous and respected paleontologists in the world. He is a member of the Paleontological Research Institute and Society of Vertebrate Paleontology and is the winner of the prestigious Katherine Palmer Award for his work communicating dinosaur and fossil information with children and communities. He has given over 300 school presentations around the country.

He is also the author of *The Complete Guide to Michigan Fossils* and *Hidden Dinosaurs.*

About Wendy Caszatt-Allen

Wendy Caszatt-Allen is an author, poet, playwright, and teacher. She is a graduate from the prestigious Interlochen Center for the Arts and Michigan State University. She is currently finishing her PhD in Language, Literacy, and Culture at the University of Iowa.

She is releasing *The Adventures of Pachelot: The Last Voyage of the Griffon* and *The Beaver Wars* in early 2007 with Mackinac Island Press.